THIS ADVENTURE
BELONGS TO

_____

Deep in the forest, in a cave by a stream,
Was a *BIG BROWN BEAR* sleeping, deep in a dream.
He'd slept snoring soundly, as leaves turned to red,
And all that time watching, lay *BAT* in her bed.

She waited and wondered, *HOW LONG* it would take, For sleepy Brown Bear, to sit up and *WAKE?*

For *TREES...*

...and the *BREEZE*

Had caused a big *BOULDER* to crash through the *ROOF*!

Now they were trapped, she would rescue Brown Bear.
She'd plotted her route, an *ADVENTURE* to share!
She needed to wake him; she'd count back from eight...

Seven, six, five, four, three, two, one and...

WAAAAAAAAKE!

He sat up quite startled, his arms moving slow,
Then seeing the boulder, he whispered, "*OH NO!*"
"Hello," said the bat, "Don't you worry, I'm here.
I've found our *ESCAPE*, there is nothing to fear!"

The bear hugged his blanket and curled in a ball,
"I'm sorry, but really? You're awfully...*SMALL!*"
The bat, smiled widely and reached for his paw,
"Come, follow me, just through this back door!"

Bear followed Bat feeling down on his luck,
He felt a bit scared, and then he got *STUCK!*

SQUEEZING
...and WHEEZING
...and WEDGING
...and POP!

PANTING
...and SQUIDGING
...and SQUISHING
...and FLOP!

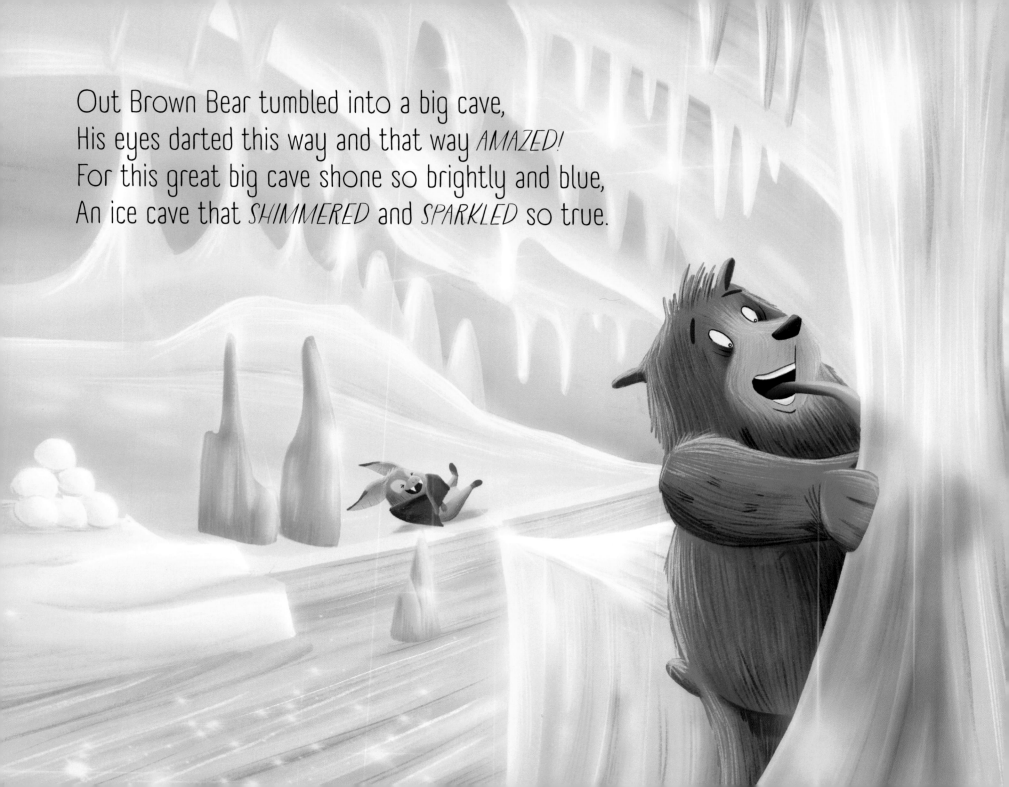

Out Brown Bear tumbled into a big cave,
His eyes darted this way and that way *AMAZED!*
For this great big cave shone so brightly and blue,
An ice cave that *SHIMMERED* and *SPARKLED* so true.

He glided and skated, his eyes open *WIDE*,
Whilst Bat slid behind him enjoying the ride.

The next cave was tiny with owls *TWIT TWOOOOO!*
And *RATS* in the next one, yes more than a few!

The next cave was *HUGE*,
with a hole to the sky.
And out shone the *MOON*,
and the *STARS* twinkling high.

Out of the corner of big Brown Bear's eye,
He noticed that Bat never once tried to *FLY.*
"Small Bat, can I ask why you don't use your wings?"
She stopped and considered, then smiling, she grinned.

"I once lived in Bat Town, I had lots of friends.
But what happened next,
who you ask it depends.
They all lived so strangely...
they hung *UPSIDE DOWN!*
But no, not for me, I like walking around!"

If we were flying, they'd go on ahead.
But I would be swooping,
ZIG-ZAGGING instead.
I knew I felt different so Bat Town I left,
And now I live here and...
...well aren't you impressed?!"

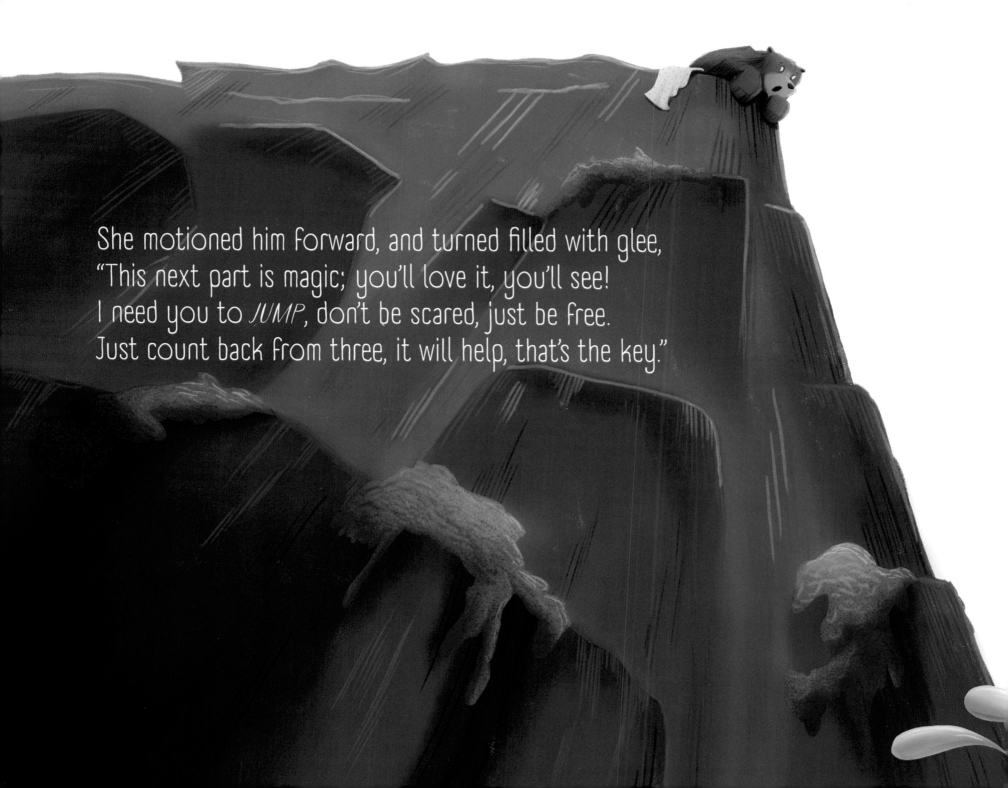

She motioned him forward, and turned filled with glee,
"This next part is magic; you'll love it, you'll see!
I need you to *JUMP*, don't be scared, just be free.
Just count back from three, it will help, that's the key."

Brown Bear was certain the bat had gone *MAD*,
Jump into the darkness, no thank you comrade!
But without a warning, as quick as a *FLASH*,
She launched herself off and then...

...and then *SPLASH!*

Gulping, he went to the edge, *THREE, TWO, ONE!*
He launched himself off and nothing could be done.
He fell and he dropped with his heart in his chest,
Then plummeting into deep water...

...the *BESTTT!*

Waving to Bear, Small Bat was quite proud,
Her rescue was big, it was *WOW*, it was loud!
Her mouth full of laughter and giggles and squeals,
She said to Brown Bear...

"WATCH OUT FOR
THE EELS!"

They floated on through a long tunnel that *GLITTERED*,
Like tiny black diamonds that *SHIMMERED* and *FLICKERED*.

Then onto the last cave, so dark yet so bright,
A million *GLOW WORMS* creating warm light!

With all the adventure they started to tire,
So Small Bat decided to build a warm fire.
They stood at the edge of the end of the cave,
And Bear said to Bat, "You've helped me be... *BRAVE!*"

"Thank you, Small Bat, For someone quite small,
You're *FIERCE* and *EXCITING*, yes, you've got it all!
Please take me to Bat Town, I want them to see,
THAT BEING YOURSELF IS
THE BEST THING TO BE!"

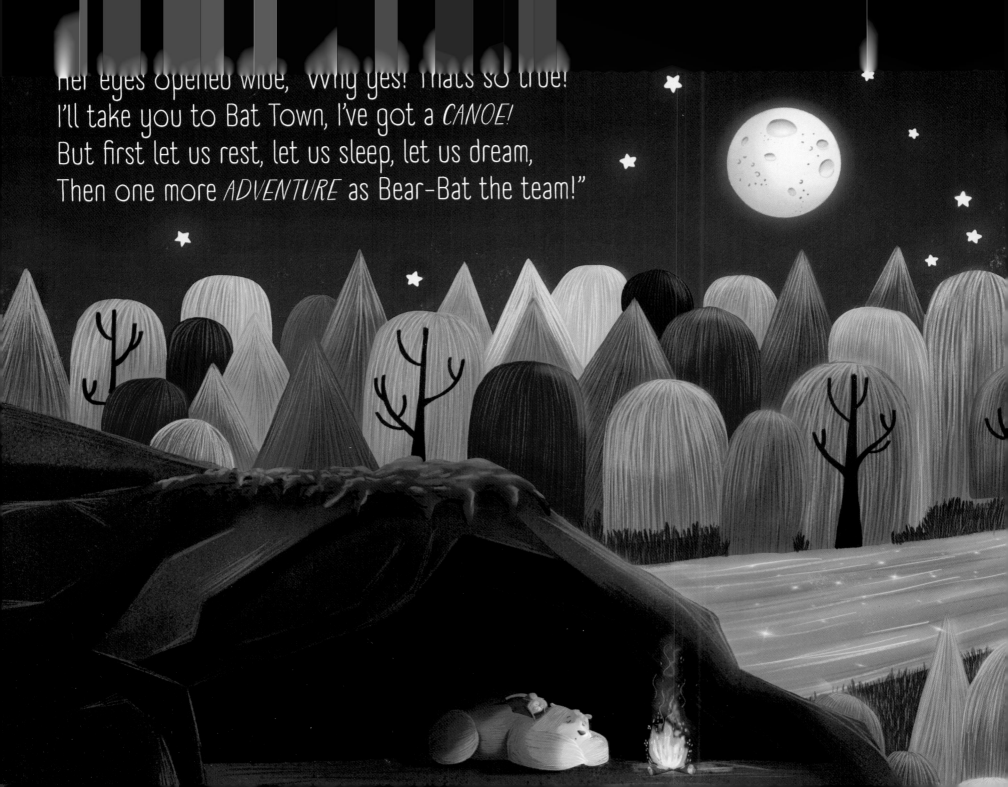

Her eyes opened wide, "Why yes! That's so true!
I'll take you to Bat Town, I've got a *CANOE!*
But first let us rest, let us sleep, let us dream,
Then one more *ADVENTURE* as Bear-Bat the team!"

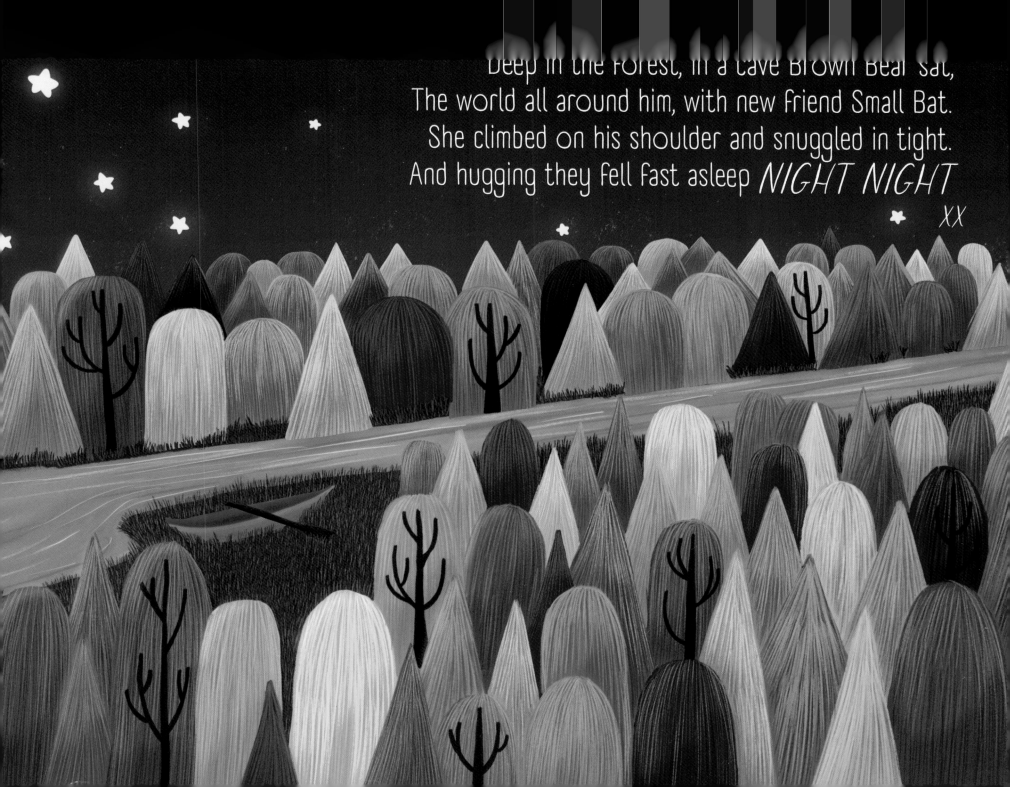

Deep in the forest, in a cave Brown Bear sat,
The world all around him, with new friend Small Bat.
She climbed on his shoulder and snuggled in tight.
And hugging they fell fast asleep *NIGHT NIGHT*

XX

This isn't the last you've seen of this pair,
There's one more *ADVENTURE* that they need to share!
Bat needs to lead them, up, down and around,
So come, join us soon, as they head to *BAT TOWN*!

Kirsty Duncan is a new children's book author, living in Cheshire, UK with her husband Adam, daughter Pippa and two cats Nala and Mowgli.

She has a First Class Bachelor of Arts Honours degree in Creative Writing and Psychology, with a number of exciting books in the pipeline.

When Kirsty isn't writing stories she enjoys chocolate, travelling, chocolate, being out in nature, chocolate, bouldering, chocolate or partaking in a quintessential British afternoon tea. And chocolate.

She also enjoys chocolate.

The thing she loves most about writing is developing the rhythm and rhyme. She also loves her words being brought to life by the amazing illustrators she works with, such as Gabika.

Gabika Collins is a children's illustrator living in sunny Australia with her three cheeky children, two happy pups and one terrific hubby.

When she is not drawing and living in her imagination, Gabika teaches water safety and swimming lessons to kids and those that are kids at heart. She loves being in the water.

She also loves reading, playing with her kids, strolling around in nature, eating at all times of the day, riding her bike and singing lyrics to songs wrong.

Her favourite thing about art and illustrating is letting her imagination run wild, and making people smile with her pictures.

Pipsy Moon Press

For Adsy, for always believing in me - KD
For Zoe, Harris and Meika, for sparking my imagination - GC

First published by Pipsy Moon Press, 2023

ISBN 978-1-7384062-1-0

Follow Kirsty @kirstyduncanwrites
Follow Gabika @bika.nella

A special thank you to our:
Chief Test Readers: Laura, Chase, Alex, Tess, Nat, Abbey, Tabby, Frankie, Max, Abbey, Louis, Chris, Libby, Rowan, Hannah and Louie
Chief Advisers: Karen Winward, Lauren Fennemore, Louise Jordan
Chief Checker of Things: Karen Winward
Chief Coaches: Adam Duncan, Claire Jerome

BV - #0104 - 091123 - C30 - 216/279/2 - PB - 9781738406210 - Gloss Lamination